Ali Daba

and the Forty Thieves

illustrated by **Claudia Venturini**

Child's Play (International) Ltd

Swindon   Auburn ME   Sydney

© 2008 Child's Play (International) Ltd   Printed in China

ISBN 978-1-84643-251-4

1 3 5 7 9 10 8 6 4 2

www.childs-play.com

Once upon a time, a poor woodcutter called Ali Baba lived in a country ruled by a band of fierce robbers. They stole from everyone, rich or poor.

One day, Ali Baba was loading wood, when he heard the noise of hooves coming through the forest. Quickly, he hid in some thick bushes.

He counted forty robbers, all on horseback.
Their leader jumped off her horse, and walked
up to a large rock.
"Open, Sesame!" she called in a loud voice.
To Ali Baba's amazement, the rock swung open!
The robbers followed the leader into a dark cave,
each of them carrying a heavy sack.

After a while, they all came out, empty-handed.

"Shut, Sesame!" cried the leader, and the cave was hidden once more. Ali Baba stayed still as stone, until all the thieves had ridden away.

Creeping out of the bushes and up to the rock, he whispered, "Open, Sesame!"
The rock swung open, and Ali Baba tiptoed into the cave.

The cave was lit from a hole in the roof, and Ali Baba was amazed to see it was filled with gold jugs and silver chests. There were bales of silk and bags of money littering the floor.

He loaded as much as he could onto his donkey, and made his escape.

"What on earth have you done?" wailed his wife, when he arrived home. "Are you in some kind of trouble? I've never seen so many fine things!" "I've taken them back from the robbers," explained Ali Baba. "We can return them to their rightful owners. But first, we have to hide them from the thieves!"

While they were burying the treasure, Ali Baba's brother, Kassim, came home. To keep him quiet, Ali Baba had to tell him the secret of where he had found it.

Very early next morning, Kassim set off secretly for the robbers' cave. He planned to take some of the treasure for himself.

Kassim loaded up all his donkeys with many fine things. But when it was time to leave, he could not remember the magic word to open the rock!

At nightfall, the robbers came back to the cave. When they found Kassim, they made him unload his donkeys. Then they locked him in a cage, to frighten off anyone else who might try to break into the cave.

When Kassim did not come home, Ali Baba began to worry.

"I hope he's not gone to the robbers' cave," he said to his wife. "I'd better go and find him."

Ali Baba set off with his donkey, and found Kassim imprisoned in the cave. He set him free at once, and put him on the back of his donkey – with a little more of the robber's treasure, of course!

"We must hide you as well," he whispered, "lest the robbers come after you!"

The robbers were amazed to find Kassim gone –
and yet more treasure missing!
"We must send a spy into the town," ordered
the leader. "Someone must know about this!"

As the spy crept around the town, he spotted
Kassim hiding in Ali Baba's house. He marked
the house in red chalk, so that he could lead
the robbers to it.

But Ali Baba's servant girl, called Marjenah, saw the robber marking the house. She suspected he was up to no good. She found a piece of red chalk, and marked all the other houses with an X as well!

The robbers crept into town, one by one, and met up with the spy. But he could not remember which was the right house, because they were all marked with red chalk!

"You're useless!" shouted the leader, "I don't want you in my gang any more!" Then she chose another robber to try to find Kassim.

As before, the second spy found Kassim.
This time, he marked the house with green chalk.
But Marjenah was watching again, and marked all
the other houses in the street as well.

"I don't believe it!" said the leader to the second spy.
"Off you go!   I'm going to have to do this myself!"

Once the leader found out where Kassim was hiding, she told her band to saddle their donkeys with two large jars each. She made each of them climb into a jar, and fastened the tops tightly.
"As soon as you hear me shout," she explained, "Jump out of the jar, and teach this man a lesson!"

Then she filled
a single jar with oil,
and set off for the town.

She knocked loudly on Ali Baba's door.

"Excuse me, sir," she explained. "I have come to sell oil at tomorrow's market, and I need a place to stay. Can you help?"

"You can stay here," Ali Baba offered. "Take the donkeys into the yard, and I will ask my servant to prepare your room. Marjenah, please fetch some oil and refill the lights."

As Marjenah crossed the yard, she overheard the robbers in the jars, whispering to each other.

At once, she saw through the plot. Quickly, she ran out into the street, and picked up a large rock, which she placed silently on top of one of the jars. Then, one by one, she did the same for all the other jars.

"You have saved our lives," Ali Baba thanked Marjenah. "And so I grant you your freedom."

"But I like it here," she replied. "Can I stay?"

"Of course," agreed Ali Baba. "This will always be your home as long as you want. Now, will you come with me to the robber's cave? We have to find out who all this treasure belongs to."

"Let's go!" Marjenah replied.
"I'll bring my chalk!"

In the middle of the night, the robber chief
rose from her bed, and crept out into the yard.

"Wake up!" she shouted at the top of her voice.
"Let's teach this fellow a lesson!"

The robbers woke up at once. They tried to jump
out of the jars, but only banged their heads! When
she saw that her plot had failed, the robber chief
took to her heels, and was never seen again.

All the noise woke Ali Baba. With the help of
the townspeople, he rolled the thieves in the jars
straight to prison, and put them safely behind bars.